Linda,

How wonderful you are!

Martha Hannah

x Yanny Darrell

Maid Martha Tells It All®

The Ghost of Hampton Court

By
Martha Hannah

Illustrated By
Larry Dowell

The First Book of
The Maid Martha Tells It All® Series

CicadaSun®
Austin, Texas

Published by CicadaSun
Austin, Texas
www.cicadasun.com

Printed in China

Jacket illustration copyright © 2006 Larry Dowell
Book design and production by CicadaSun.

Publisher's Cataloging-in-Publication
(Provided by Quality Books, Inc.)

Hannah, Martha.
   The ghost of Hampton Court / by Martha Hannah ; illustrated by Larry Dowell.
   p. cm. -- (Maid Martha tells it all series; 1st bk.)
   SUMMARY: Maid Martha, a Medieval storyteller, recounts the marriage of King Henry VIII to the teenager Catharine Howard. The sixteenth century English king accuses Catharine of treason and has her beheaded. Her tormented ghost is said to still haunt Hampton Court Palace.
   LCCN 2006925320
   ISBN 0-9779808-0-4

   1. Henry VIII, King of England, 1491-1547--Juvenile fiction. 2. Catharine Howard, Queen, consort of Henry VIII, King of England, d. 1542--Juvenile fiction. 3. Hampton Court (Richmond upon Thames, London, England)--Juvenile fiction. 4. Ghosts--Juvenile fiction. 5. Great Britain--History--Henry VIII, 1509-1547--Juvenile fiction. 6. Historical fiction. [1. Henry VIII, King of England, 1491-1547--Fiction. 2. Catharine Howard, Queen, consort of Henry VIII, King of England, d. 1542--Fiction. 3. Hampton Court (Richmond upon Thames, London, England)--Fiction. 4. Ghosts--Fiction. 5. Haunted places--Fiction. 6. Kings, queens, rulers, etc.--Fiction. 7. Great Britain--History--Henry VIII, 1509-1547--Fiction.] I. Dowell, Larry. II. Title. III. Series.

PZ7.H1976Gho 2006   [Fic]
                   QBI06-600275

To my wonderful and hilarious father, Comer Hannah, Jr.
and in memory, my charming and sweet mother,
Nellie Nichols Hannah for their constant love,
encouragement and unfailing belief in me.
– M. H.

To my brother, Jerry – I wish you and your easy laugh
were still with us.
– L. D.

For all the encouragement and kind advice,
special thanks go to:
Connie Edwards, Lisa Youngblood, Janette Johnston,
Rosalind Eyre, Kassandra Garcia, Lucas Miller,
Carol Tucker Mills, Dianne de Las Casa and
our Court Jester in Crime, Eddie Nichols.
– M. H. & L. D.

There once was a king, a king of England. He was king as was his father before him. His last name was Tudor and he lived during the late Middle Ages. Now, this king of England was very powerful and he was mean. He was so mean...

You're supposed to say, "How mean was he?"

This king of England was so mean that the more he wanted, the more he got. And the more he got, the more he wanted. For he was king. Early on, as a child, this king became very spoiled. And when he grew up, he was so spoiled that the more he wanted, the more he got. And got and got and got. And the more he got, the more powerful he became.

His subjects loved him, this king of England, but they feared him. In particular, because he was so powerful and so mean. He was so mean...

You're supposed to say, "How mean was he?"

He was so mean that he had many wives. When he got tired of a wife or angry at a wife, he would have her head chopped off. Do you know what king I'm talking about?

That's right! Henry! Henry the Eighth, King of England.

See, Henry had six wives in all. And two lost their heads. If a wife disagreed with him or did not do as he liked, he would call her a traitor and send her off to be punished. And, most likely, beheaded.

The first wife Henry married for power and love. The second had a shrewish bad temper which earned her a one-way boat ride to the chopping block! But that was not before the king had his eye set on yet another wife. And on it went.

Now Henry the Eighth was very mean. He was so mean...

Come on! You're supposed to say, "How mean was he?"

Henry the Eighth was so mean that he had many castles, and yet he put a man in jail in order to get a castle. He put Cardinal Wolsey in jail in order to get Hampton Court. Cardinal Wolsey was head of the Catholic Church in England. He was so rich and powerful that he had Hampton Court built.

And I'm telling you now, it's not wise to become more powerful than the king. Not least of all this king. Someone should've told Cardinal Wolsey! So, Henry the Eighth sent Cardinal Wolsey to jail, to prison and that is where Cardinal Wolsey died.

Oh, all right, it was on the way to jail, but indeed, he died.

Have you ever been to England? Have you ever been to Hampton Court? If you have, then you know. It's a glorious castle that sits right on the banks of the River Thames. It's surrounded by wonderful gardens filled with beautiful roses as far as you can see.

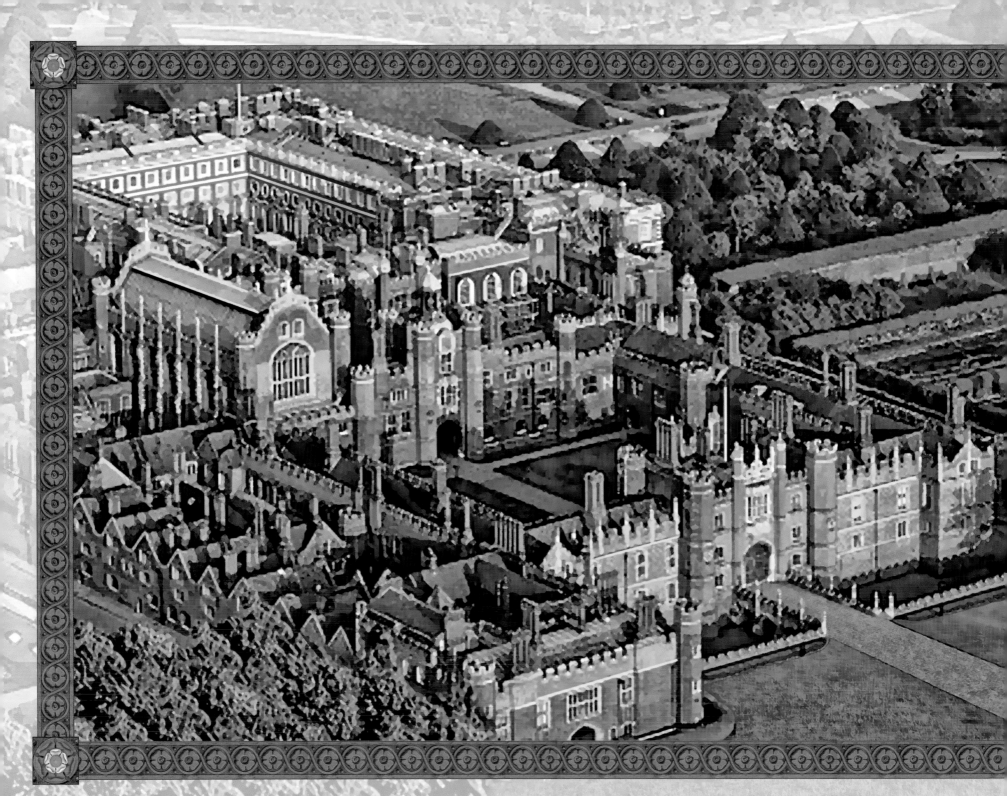

Oh, and the castle, my! It is enormous! It's room after room after room. You could walk all day and not see it all. It's more like a small city, it is. When Henry the Eighth lived there, it was even larger.

When Henry the Eigth lived at Hampton Court, he met and married a beautiful young lady. Catharine Howard was her name. And once King Henry set his eyes on her, she was to become his wife, whether she liked it or no. For if this powerful king wanted to marry you, he married you. For he was king!

Catharine Howard became his fifth wife and Queen of England. See, it goes with the job if you marry a king...

Henry and Catharine were happy for a time. But do you think it lasted long?

Oh, no! You see, King Henry got restless. He accused her of being in love with someone else. And she may very well have been. For you see, the king was much older, had a gouty leg...

Do you know how old Catharine was when they got married? She was only 15 years old! See, gossip got out that Catharine was in love with someone else. Maybe it was her music teacher. Maybe it was someone she'd loved before she got married. Maybe it was someone she'd loved when she had no choice but to marry Henry.

And, gossip being what it is and as powerful as it is, in time it found its way to Henry. King Henry brought in a judge and a jury and had a trial. And, Catharine was tried for treason. "Traitor! Traitor! For what else could she be", they all said, pointing fingers, "if she is not loyal to the king?"

Now, who do you think won? Ah, the king of course. For he was king! Poor Catharine was doomed. There was no way she could win.

Catherine Howard was put in her chambers under house arrest. The day would come that she would be taken away to be punished. On the day she was to be taken away, the guards came to Queen Catharine's chambers. They took her by her arms.

And, on that day of all days, Henry the Eighth was kneeling in prayer in the Royal Chapel. Henry the Eighth kneeling in prayer! Ha!

Well, it was a big joke back then...

The guards took Catharine by her arms, but she broke free. She ran from her chambers down a long hallway, the long hallway that leads to the Royal Chapel doors. She was begging and pleading, "Henry, please! No! You know I'm innocent! Please!" But, do you know, he did not even turn around. He ignored her entirely!

The guards grabbed her again, roughly this time. They took Queen Catharine by her arms and dragged her down that long hallway that leads from the Royal Chapel doors. She was taken out the many courtyards of Hampton Court. She was put on a boat right there on the River Thames.

Catherine took that long boat ride down the River Thames, a boat ride you can take today. She was taken to the Tower of London, a castle you can visit today.

And there at the castle, the Tower of London, she was taken through the Traitor's Gate, better yet known as the Weeping Gate, for indeed, she was weeping.

And at the Tower of London Queen Catharine was held prisoner. Within the week, she was taken to the courtyard, then marched to the chopping block, where she was beheaded. Her head was chopped off!

Now, late at night, if you find yourself at Hampton Court; if you find yourself at Hampton Court after all the visitors have gone and everyone's gone to sleep; if you find yourself in that long hallway that leads to the Royal Chapel doors... You'll see her, you will! It's a young lady appears, dressed in white.

And, she not walks, but floats! Down that long hallway begging and moaning and pleading, "Please, Henry, no! You know I'm innocent! Please!"

And when she gets to the Royal Chapel doors, she raises her arms up in anguish and SCREAMS!

And then she disappears!

And that's the true story of the Ghost of Hampton Court!

Interesting Historical Facts from the Tudor Age of Henry VIII

1491 Henry VIII was born the son of King Henry VII. As a child, Henry was so spoiled he had a 'whipping boy' to take his punishment or whippings in his stead when he got in trouble.

1509 Henry became King and married Catherine of Aragon, mother of Mary.

1533 Henry divorced Catherine to marry Ann Boleyn, mother of Elizabeth.

1536 Henry married Jane Seymour eleven days after Ann's beheading. She gave birth to his only son, Edward and died from childbirth soon after.

1540 An arranged marriage, Henry married and quickly divorced Ann of Cleaves, who was not at all to his liking. She was glad at that. Saved her neck, it did.

1540 Henry VIII married Catharine Howard, whose life was short and sweet with a far-reaching tragic end. In 1542, when Catharine was sentenced to the 'block', several close family members, servants, a past fiancé, and another said-to-be love were imprisoned, tortured, hanged and beheaded.

1547 Henry VIII died at age 56. Catherine Parr, whom he married three years earlier, outlived him, much to her relief.

1515 Hampton Court was transformed into a grand palace from an ancient manor house and estate by Cardinal Wolsey, Cardinal-Archbishop of York and Lord Chancellor of England.

1528 Henry VIII took as his own, rebuilt and remodeled Hampton Court Palace. He filled it with endless royal apartments, waiting, sitting and eating chambers, hallways, kitchens, the Great Hall and the amazing Royal Chapel.

Hampton Court Palace gardens included tennis courts, bowling greens and a huge hedge maze designed just for fun. You can get lost in the maze. I certainly have. The hedge is a puzzle. You have to figure it out.

The Tower of London was the castle where King Henry VIII sent many of his family, friends and advisors to be punished, tortured and beheaded. It was risky to be close to the king.

If you were to be executed at the Tower of London, you had to pay the executioner money. It was part of your punishment. Executioners could be as young as 16 years old.